LAUGH
-Out-
LOUD
CHRISTMAS
JOKES
for KIDS

LAUGH -Out- LOUD CHRISTMAS JOKES for KIDS

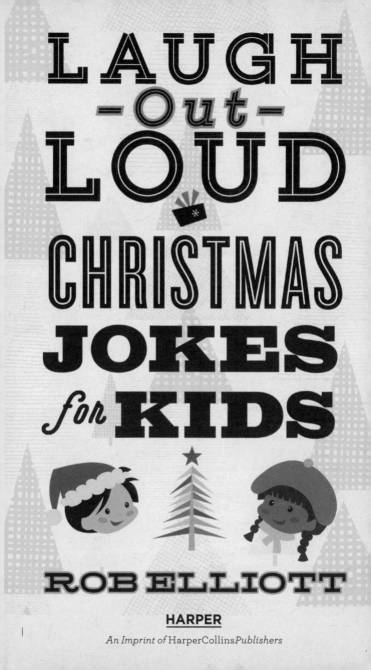

ROB ELLIOTT

HARPER

An Imprint of HarperCollinsPublishers

ISBN 978-0-06-249791-8

Typography by Gearbox
16 17 18 19 20   PC/BRR   10 9 8 7 6 5 4 3 2 1
❖
First Edition

To my mother, Maribeth, and my dad, Robert (1937–2012): You gave me a deep love for the holidays and taught me the true meaning of Christmas.

With all my heart,

Rob

- -

Q: What did the Christmas tree say to the ornament?

A: "Quit hanging around."

Q: What do snowmen eat for lunch?

A: Brrrr-itos

Q: Where does Santa keep his money?

A: In a snowbank

Q: What is a Christmas tree's least favorite month of the year?

A: Sep-timber

- -

Q: What do you get when you mix a dog with a snowflake?

A: Frostbite

Q: Why did Santa feel bad about himself?

A: Because he had low elf-esteem.

Q: Why don't lobsters give Christmas presents?

A: Because they're shellfish.

Q: What do you call a cat who gives you presents?

A: Santa Paws

- -

Q: What did Frosty wear to the wedding?

A: His snowsuit

Q: What is Jack Frost's favorite movie?

A: *The Blizzard of Oz*

Knock, knock.

Who's there?

Peas.

Peas who?

Peas tell me what you're giving me

for Christmas!

Knock, knock.

Who's there?

Norway.

Norway who?

There is Norway I'm kissing anybody

under the mistletoe!

- -

Q: What is the coldest month of the year?

A: Decemb-rrrrr

Q: What is a tiger's favorite Christmas song?

A: "Jungle Bells"

Q: Why was Santa dressed up?

A: Because he was going to the snowball.

Q: Why do snowmen always change their minds?

A: Because they're flaky!

Q: Where do elves go to vote?

A: The North Poll

Q: Where does the Easter Bunny get his eggs at Christmastime?

A: From the three French hens

Q: What does Santa give Rudolph when he has bad breath?

A: Orna-mints

Q: What do snowmen wear on their feet?

A: Snowshoes

Knock, knock.

Who's there?

Freeze.

Freeze who?

Freeze a Jolly Good Fellow.

Q: Who brings Christmas presents to a shark?

A: Santa Jaws

Q: What's a polar bear's favorite cereal?

A: Ice Krispies

Knock, knock.

Who's there?

Hugo.

Hugo who?

Hugo sit on Santa's lap first, then I'll go second.

Knock, knock.

Who's there?

Dubai.

Dubai who?

I'm off Dubai some Christmas presents for you!

Knock, knock.

Who's there?

Butter.

Butter who?

You butter watch out. You butter not cry. You butter not pout I'm telling you why. . . .

Knock, knock.

Who's there?

Elf.

Elf who?

Elf finish wrapping the presents right away!

Q: What always falls at Christmas but never gets hurt?

A: Snow!

Santa: Elf, I have something to tell you.

Elf: I'm all ears.

Q: Why does Rudolph's nose shine at night?

A: Because he's a light sleeper.

- -

Q: What did the gingerbread man do when he sprained his ankle?

A: He iced it.

Q: What do elves post on Facebook?

A: Elf-ies

Q: What do gingerbread men do before they go to bed?

A: Change their cookie sheets

Q: How do frogs celebrate Christmas?

A: They kiss under the mistle-toad.

Q: How do snowmen carry their books to school?

A: In their snowpacks

Q: What do grumpy sheep say during the holidays?

A: "Baa, baa, humbug."

Q: What is a sheep's favorite Christmas song?

A: "Fleece Navidad"

Knock, knock.

Who's there?

Canoe.

Canoe who?

Canoe help me put up the Christmas tree?

- -

Knock, knock.

Who's there?

Wooden shoe.

Wooden shoe who?

Wooden shoe like to know what you're getting for Christmas?

Knock, knock.

Who's there?

Waldo.

Waldo who?

Waldo we do to celebrate New Year's Eve?

Q: Why do elves go to school?

A: To learn the elf-abet

- -

Q: Why can't a Christmas tree learn to knit?

A: Because they always drop their needles.

Q: Why doesn't Santa let the elves use his computer?

A: They always delete the Christmas cookies.

Q: What is Santa's favorite kind of sandwich?

A: Peanut butter and jolly

Q: What is a penguin's favorite kind of cereal?

A: Frosted Flakes

Q: Where do Santa's reindeer stop for coffee?

A: Star-bucks

Knock, knock.

Who's there?

Myrrh.

Myrrh who?

Myrrh Christmas and a Happy New Year!

Knock, knock.

Who's there?

Udder.

Udder who?

Udder the tree you'll find your present!

Q: What do fish sing at Christmastime?

A: Christmas corals

Q: What do ducks like to eat at

Christmas parties?

A: Cheese and quackers

Knock, knock.

Who's there?

Ya.

Ya who?

Wow, ya really excited about Christmas!

Knock, knock.

Who's there?

Iva.

Iva who?

Iva bunch of decorations to put on the tree.

- -

Knock, knock.

Who's there?

Avenue.

Avenue who?

Avenue started your Christmas shopping yet?

Knock, knock.

Who's there?

Cannoli.

Cannoli who?

I cannoli eat one more Christmas cookie!

Q: Why did Santa pay top dollar for a box of candy canes?

A: Because they were in MINT condition!

Q: What goes *ho, ho, ho, thump*?

A: Santa laughing his head off!

- -

Q: What do you call a snowman who vacations in Florida?

A: A puddle

Knock, knock.

Who's there?

Snow.

Snow who?

I snow what Santa's bringing you for Christmas.

Knock, knock.

Who's there?

Snowman.

Snowman who?

Snowman has ever seen Santa's workshop at the North Pole.

- -

Q: What do you get when you cross a pinecone and a polar bear?

A: A fur tree

Q: Why did the math teacher get sick after Christmas dinner?

A: He had too much pi.

Q: What is an elf's favorite part of school?

A: Snow-and-tell

Q: What do you get when you combine a Christmas tree and an iPod?

A: A pineapple

Knock, knock.

Who's there?

Whale.

Whale who?

Whale, I can't believe the holidays are almost here!

Q: What does an elf listen to on the radio?

A: Wrap music

Q: Why doesn't Santa hide presents in the closet?

A: He has Claus-trophobia.

Knock, knock.

Who's there?

Dexter.

Dexter who?

Dexter halls with boughs of holly!

Q: How do snowmen spend their Christmas vacations?

A: Chilling out

Knock, knock.

Who's there?

Arthur.

Arthur who?

Arthur any more Christmas presents to open?

Q: **What does Santa give his reindeer for a stomachache?**

A: Elk-a-Seltzer

Q: **What do gingerbread men use when they break their legs?**

A: Candy canes

Q: **What is green, white, and red all over?**

A: An elf with sunburn

Q: **Why didn't the rope get any presents?**

A: Because it was knotty.

Q: **What did Mrs. Claus say to Rudolph when he was grumpy?**

A: "You need to lighten up!"

Q: How much did Santa pay for his reindeer?

A: A few bucks

Q: Why did the gingerbread man go to the doctor?

A: He was feeling crumb-y!

Q: What is something you can throw during the holidays but never catch?

A: A Christmas party

Q: Why doesn't Santa ever have spare change?

A: Because he's Jolly Old St. Nickel-less.

Q: How does a polar bear write out his Christmas list?

A: With a pen-guin

- -

Q: Why was the cat put on Santa's naughty list?

A: Because he was a cheat-ah.

Q: How did the orange get into the Christmas stocking?

A: It squeezed its way in!

Knock, knock.

Who's there?

Annie.

Annie who?

Annie-body want some Christmas cookies?

Q: Why was the cat afraid to climb the Christmas tree?

A: It was scared of the bark!

Q: Why did Santa carry a giant sponge while delivering presents in Florida?

A: He wanted to soak up the sun!

Q: Why did Santa have a clock in his sleigh?

A: He wanted to watch time fly.

Q: How did the pony break its Christmas present?

A: It wouldn't stop horsing around.

Q: Why did the baker give everybody free cookies for Christmas?

A: Because he had a lot of dough!

Knock, knock.

Who's there?

Donut.

Donut who?

I donut know how Santa gets down the chimney on Christmas Eve!

Knock, knock.

Who's there?

Justin.

Justin who?

You're Justin time for Christmas carols.

Knock, knock.

Who's there?

Willie.

Willie who?

Willie keep his New Year's resolution this year?

- -

Knock, knock.

Who's there?

Oldest.

Oldest who?

**Oldest Christmas shopping is giving
me a headache!**

Knock, knock.

Who's there?

Snow place.

Snow place who?

There's snow place like home.

**Q: What does the Easter Bunny like to drink
during the holidays?**

A: Eggnog

Knock, knock.

Who's there?

Nutella.

Nutella who?

There's Nutella what Santa might bring for Christmas this year.

Rita: What time is it when a polar bear sits in your chair?

Adam: I'm not sure.

Rita: It's time to get a new chair.

Knock, knock.

Who's there?

Water.

Water who?

Water you doing for New Year's Eve?

Q: Why is Santa so good at gardening?

A: Because he likes to hoe, hoe, hoe.

Knock, knock.

Who's there?

Tibet.

Tibet who?

Go Tibet early tonight, because Santa is coming!

Q: What did the astronaut get for Christmas?

A: A launch box

Q: What is a skunk's favorite Christmas song?

A: "Jingle Smells"

Knock, knock.

Who's there?

Juicy.

Juicy who?

Juicy all the pretty Christmas lights?

Knock, knock.

Who's there?

Rabbit.

Rabbit who?

Rabbit up with paper and ribbon, and put it under the tree.

Q: What kind of motorcycle does Santa drive?

A: A Holly Davidson

- -

Knock, knock.

Who's there?

Quiche.

Quiche who?

Quiche me under the mistletoe!

Knock, knock.

Who's there?

Jester.

Jester who?

In jester minute it'll be the New Year!

Q: What's a mermaid's favorite

Christmas story?

A: *A Christmas Coral*

Q: What did the rattlesnakes do at their Christmas party?

A: They hissed under the mistletoe.

Q: What do elves use to wash their hands?

A: Santa-tizer

Q: What do you call it when people are afraid of Santa?

A: Claus-trophobic

Q: What do boxers like to drink at Christmas parties?

A: Punch!

Knock, knock.

Who's there?

Yule.

Yule who?

Yule really like your Christmas present this year.

Knock, knock.

Who's there?

Anna.

Anna who?

Anna partridge in a pear tree.

Q: How did the crab wish his mom a Merry Christmas?

A: He called her on his shell phone.

Q: Why does a cat take so long to wrap Christmas presents?

A: He won't stop until they're purr-fect.

Q: Why did Santa go buy more reindeer?

A: They were on sale and didn't cost much doe!

Q: Why did the elf have to stay after school?

A: He was in trouble for losing his gnome-work.

Knock, knock.

Who's there?

Roach.

Roach who?

I roach you a letter to wish you Merry Christmas!

Q: How does Frosty get around?

A: On his ice-cycle

Q: What do pigs use to write their Christmas list for Santa?

A: A pig pen

Q: How do elves learn to chop down a Christmas tree?

A: They go to boarding school.

Q: Why did the Christmas tree go to bed early?

A: It was bushed!

Q: What does Frosty do when he feels stressed out?

A: He takes a chill pill.

Q: Why was the chicken put on Santa's naughty list?

A: It kept laying deviled eggs.

Q: What do you get when you cross a lobster and Santa?

A: Santa Claws

Knock, knock.

Who's there?

Arthur.

Arthur who?

My Arthur-ritis is acting up from the winter weather.

Q: What is Santa's favorite singer?

A: Elf-is Presley

Knock, knock.

Who's there?

Wart.

Wart who?

Wart is your favorite Christmas carol?

Q: What do you call a snowman's kids?

A: Chilled-ren

Q: What did the one penguin say to the other?

A: "Ice to meet you."

Q: What's a dinosaur's least favorite reindeer?

A: Comet

Q: What do polar bears wear on their heads?

A: Snowcaps

Q: What do penguins use in science class?

A: Beak-ers

Q: What did the candy cane say to the ornament?

A: "Hang in there."

Q: What do you call it when the elves take a break?

A: A Santa pause

George: Whose music is best for decking the halls?

James: A-wreath-a Franklin's!

- -

Q: How does the alphabet change during the holidays?

A: The Christmas alphabet has noel.

Knock, knock.

Who's there?

Owl.

Owl who?

Owl always love to celebrate Christmas.

Q: What is Santa Claus's nationality?

A: North Polish

Knock, knock.

Who's there?

Alba.

Alba who?

Alba home for Christmas.

Knock, knock.

Who's there?

Wayne.

Wayne who?

A Wayne a manger.

Josh: Do you know how much Santa paid for his sleigh and reindeer?

Jeff: Maybe a few bucks?

Josh: Nothing! It was on the house.

Q: What do you call a polar bear in the Caribbean?

A: Lost!

Q: **What did the chicken have to do after eating all the Christmas cookies?**

A: Egg-cercise

Knock, knock.

Who's there?

Uno.

Uno who?

Uno Christmas is a season for giving.

Knock, knock.

Who's there?

Latte.

Latte who?

Thanks a latte for all the Christmas presents!

- -

Q: What kind of cookies make Santa laugh?

A: Snickerdoodles

Q: Why wouldn't Rudolph stay in the barn?

A: Because he was un-stable.

Q: What's an elf's favorite Christmas song?

A: "I'll Be Gnome for Christmas"

Q: What does a whale write in his Christmas cards?

A: Sea-sons greetings!

Knock, knock.

Who's there?

Turnip.

Turnip who?

Turnip the Christmas music!

Q: What does Santa wear when he goes golfing?

A: A tee-shirt

Knock, knock.

Who's there?

Dishes.

Dishes who?

Dishes going to be the best Christmas we've ever had.

Q: How did the turtle behave at the Christmas party?

A: He wouldn't come out of his shell.

Knock, knock.

Who's there?

Interrupting Santa.

Interrupting San—

Ho, ho, ho!

Q: How do you know Santa is good at karate?

A: Because he wears a black belt.

Knock, knock.

Who's there?

Pasture.

Pasture who?

Pasture eggnog—I'm thirsty!

Q: Which one of Santa's reindeer likes to clean the workshop?

A: Comet

Q: **How did Santa feel when his reindeer got fleas?**

A: It really ticked him off!

Q: **What do you have in December that's not in any other month?**

A: The letter *D*

Q: **What's a mime's favorite Christmas carol?**

A: "Silent Night"

Q: **What do snowmen say when they play hide-and-seek?**

A: "I-cy you!"

Q: **What do polar bears put on their tacos?**

A: Chilly sauce

- -

Q: Why does Santa go down the chimney?

A: Because it soots him.

Q: Why does a broken drum make a great Christmas present?

A: Because you just can't beat it!

Q: Who does Frosty like to visit during the holidays?

A: His aunt Arctica

Q: What's a polar bear's favorite dinner?

A: Ham-brrrrr-gers

Tongue Twisters

Crispy Christmas cookies

Twelve twisted elves

Santa's snowy sleigh

Plump penguins

Q: Where do skunks like to sit during Christmas church service?

A: In the front pew

Q: What do you get when you cross a dinosaur and an evergreen?

A: A tree rex

Q: Why were Santa's reindeer so itchy?

A: From the antarc-ticks

Knock, knock.

Who's there?

Watson.

Watson who?

Watson your Christmas wish list this year?

Knock, knock.

Who's there?

Yoda.

Yoda who?

Yoda one I want to wish a Merry Christmas!

Knock, knock.

Who's there?

Soda.

Soda who?

It's soda-pressing that the holidays are almost over!

- -

Q: What did one iceberg say to the other?

A: "I think we're drifting apart."

Knock, knock.

　Who's there?

Ivy.

　Ivy who?

Ivy lot of Christmas cards to put in the mail!

Q: How do snowmen like their root beer?

A: In a frosted mug

Q: What did the basil say to the oregano?

A: "Seasoning's greetings."

Q: Why couldn't Jack Frost go

　Christmas shopping?

A: Because his bank account was frozen!

Sam: Did you have fun at the pig's Christmas party?

Sue: No, it was a boar.

Knock, knock.

Who's there?

Brett.

Brett who?

I Brett you don't know what's in your Christmas stocking!

Q: What do you get when you cross Santa Claus and the Easter Bunny?

A: Jolly beans

Q: How did Humpty Dumpty feel after he finished Christmas shopping?

A: Eggs-hausted

- -

Q: Why did Rudolph put his money in the freezer?

A: He wanted some cold, hard cash!

Q: Where do crocodiles keep their eggnog?

A: In the refriger-gator

Knock, knock.

Who's there?

Otter.

Otter who?

You otter come to my house for Christmas this year.

Q: Why was the owl so popular at the Christmas party?

A: He was a hoot!

Q: How do reindeer carry their oats?

A: In a buck-et

Knock, knock.

Who's there?

Nacho.

Nacho who?

It's nacho turn to open a Christmas present.

Q: Why won't snowmen eat any carrot cake?

A: They're afraid it has boogers in it.

Q: What do you get when you combine Santa Claus and Sherlock Holmes?

A: Santa Clues

- -

Q: How do Santa's reindeer know when it's time to deliver presents?

A: They check their calen-deer.

Q: Why do fishermen send Santa so many letters?

A: They love dropping him a line.

Knock, knock.

Who's there?

Bacon.

Bacon who?

I'm bacon dozens of Christmas cookies this year!

Q: Why didn't the beetle like Christmas?

A: Because he was a humbug.

- -

Q: What is Santa's favorite kind of candy?

A: Jolly Ranchers

Q: Why did Frosty get kicked out of the farmer's market?

A: He was caught picking his nose.

Q: Why wouldn't the turkey eat dessert after Christmas dinner?

A: He was too stuffed.

Q: Where do bugs like to shop for their Christmas presents?

A: At the flea market

Q: Why doesn't Santa ever worry about the past?

A: Because he's always focused on the present.

Q: What's the best state for listening to Christmas music?

A: South Carol-ina

Q: What kind of animal needs an umbrella?

A: Rain-deer

Q: What happened when Santa took a nap in the fireplace?

A: He slept like a log.

Knock, knock.

Who's there?

Acid.

Acid who?

Acid I'd stop by and bring you a Christmas present.

Q: What do you call decorations hanging from Rudolph's antlers?

A: Christmas horn-aments

Q: Why did the snowman's mouth hurt?

A: Because he had a coal sore.

Q: What do polar bears eat for lunch?

A: Iceberg-ers

Knock, knock.

Who's there?

Walnut.

Walnut who?

I walnut let the holidays go by without wishing you a Merry Christmas!

Knock, knock.

Who's there?

Muffin.

Muffin who?

Naughty kids get muffin for Christmas.

Q: Where do people sing Christmas songs quietly?

A: Bethle-hum

- -

Q: How do you find your way to the New Year's Eve party?

A: Follow the auld lang signs.

Knock, knock.

Who's there?

Les.

Les who?

Les go caroling and get some hot chocolate!

Q: What happened when the dentist didn't get a Christmas present?

A: It really hurt his fillings.

Knock, knock.

Who's there?

Mustache.

Mustache who?

I mustache you to come to my Christmas party!

Q: What do you get when you combine a penguin and a jalapeño?

A: A chilly pepper

Knock, knock.

Who's there?

Meow.

Meow who?

Meow-y Christmas!

- -

Q: How do you decorate a scientist's lab for Christmas?

A: With a chemis-tree

Knock, knock.

Who's there?

Dachshund.

Dachshund who?

Dachshund through the snow in a one-horse open sleigh.

Q: What shoes did the baker wear while baking holiday bread?

A: His loafers

Q: What kinds of trees wear gloves in the winter?

A: Palm trees

- -

Q: Why don't you want to make a

snowman angry?

A: He might have a total meltdown.

Knock, knock.

Who's there?

Dragon.

Dragon who?

I'm dragon my feet on getting my Christmas

shopping done.

Q: Who watched out for the snowman during

the blizzard?

A: His snow angel

Q: Why did the mom put her son in the corner

after he went snowboarding?

A: She wanted him to warm up in 90 degrees.

- -

Knock, knock.

Who's there?

Cole.

Cole who?

Cole goes in naughty kids' stockings.

Q: Why would you invite a mushroom to a Christmas party?

A: Because he's a fungi.

Q: What do you call a dentist who cleans the abominable snowman's teeth?

A: CRAZY!!!

Q: What do Halloween mummies and Christmas elves have in common?

A: They both have a lot of wrapping.

- -

Q: What kind of drink is never ready on time?

A: Hot choco-late

Knock, knock.

Who's there?

Butcher.

Butcher who?

Butcher arms around me and give me a kiss under the mistletoe.

Q: Why don't polar bears and penguins get along?

A: Because they're polar opposites.

Q: What do you call a cow that lives in an igloo?

A: An Eski-moo

Q: What do you call Frosty's cell phone?

A: A snow-mobile

Q: What do you give a baboon for Christmas?

A: A monkey wrench

Q: What do you give a wasp for Christmas?

A: A bee-bee gun

Q: What do squirrels have for breakfast on Christmas morning?

A: Do-nuts

- -

Q: What did the whale get in its Christmas stocking?

A: Blubber gum

Q: What do you get when Jack Frost turns on the radio?

A: Really cool music

Q: Why didn't the cow like its crummy Christmas present?

A: It was a milk dud.

Q: How do starfish celebrate the holiday season?

A: With yule-tide greetings

- -

Knock, knock.

Who's there?

Hailey.

Hailey who?

I'm Hailey a cab so we'll make it to the Christmas party on time!

Q: What do you give a lamb for Christmas?

A: A sheeping bag

Knock, knock.

Who's there?

Howie.

Howie who?

Howie going to get that big star on top of the Christmas tree?

Knock, knock.

Who's there?

Noah.

Noah who?

Noah good place to buy candy canes?

Knock, knock.

Who's there?

Taco.

Taco who?

Let's taco 'bout what we'll do for

Christmas vacation!

- -

Knock, knock.

Who's there?

Dawn.

Dawn who?

Dawn forget to leave cookies for Santa on

Christmas Eve!

Knock, knock.

Who's there?

Betty.

Betty who?

I Betty can't guess what I got him for Christmas!

Knock, knock.

Who's there?

Cold.

Cold who?

Cold you come out and build a snowman

with me?

Q: What happened to Santa when he went down the chimney?

A: He got the flue.

Q: What do you get from a cow that receives too many presents for Christmas?

A: Spoiled milk!

Knock, knock.

Who's there?

Luke.

Luke who?

Luke up in the sky for Santa's sleigh!

Knock, knock.

Who's there?

Howard.

Howard who?

Howard you like to make some Christmas cookies?

Q: How did the mad scientist cause a blizzard?

A: He was brainstorming.

Jimmy: What do you call a wreath under a pile of snow?

Joey: A holly bury

Q: Why did the librarian have to miss the Christmas party?

A: She was double-booked.

- -

Q: Why did the polar bear get glasses?

A: To improve its ice-sight (eyesight)

Q: How does an Eskimo fix his broken sled?

A: With i-glue

Q: Why did Santa sing lullabies to his sack?

A: He wanted a sleeping bag.

Q: Why did Rudolph need braces?

A: Because he had buck teeth.

- -

Q: Why did Santa use Rudolph to guide his sleigh?

A: It was a bright idea.

Q: What did one Christmas light say to the other?

A: "Do you want to go out tonight?"

Q: Why was Mrs. Claus crying?

A: She stubbed her mistletoe.

Q: Why is the Grinch so good at gardening?

A: He has a green thumb.

Q: Why was the frosting so stressed out?

A: It was spread too thin.

Q: Why wouldn't the parakeet buy his girlfriend a Christmas present?

A: Because he was cheep.

Q: Why are pigs so fun at Christmas parties?

A: Because they go hog wild.

Q: What do you call a guy whose snowmobile breaks down?

A: A cab

Q: Why don't you invite the Polar Express to dinner?

A: It always choo-choos with its mouth open.

- -

Knock, knock.

Who's there?

Raymond.

Raymond who?

Raymond me to leave out some cookies

for Santa.

Knock, knock.

Who's there?

Johanna.

Johanna who?

Johanna come out and build a snowman?

Knock, knock.

Who's there?

Duncan.

Duncan who?

Duncan cookies in hot cocoa is delicious!

- -

Q: Why wasn't a creature stirring on Christmas Eve?

A: Because they had already finished making their Christmas soup.

Joe: Did your goat eat my hat and mittens?

Jim: Yes, he scarfed them right down.

Q: What's as big as a polar bear but weighs nothing?

A: A polar bear's shadow

Q: Why wouldn't Rudolph leave the barn to guide the sleigh?

A: He was stalling.

Q: **What do porcupines say when they kiss under the mistletoe?**

A: "Ouch!"

Q: **What happened when the frog's snowmobile broke down?**

A: It had to be toad away.

Q: **What did Mrs. Claus say when Santa came home late?**

A: "Where on earth have you been?"

Q: **What did the fish think of its Christmas present?**

A: She thought it was fin-tastic!

Q: **What did Santa say when Mrs. Claus made him coffee?**

A: "Thanks a latte!"

Q: **What do you get when you cross a duck and a squirrel?**

A: A nut-quacker

Q: **What do you get when you cross a reindeer and a fish?**

A: Ru-dolphin

Q: **Why was the skunk put on Santa's naughty list?**

A: Because he was a stinker.

Jack: Why did you give me worms for Christmas?

Jeff: Because they were dirt cheap!

Q: What do you do if a polar bear is in your bed?

A: Find a hotel for the night!

Q: What do you get if you cross a turtle and a snowman?

A: A snow-poke

Q: What did the Dalmatian say after Christmas dinner?

A: "That hit the spot!"

Q: How do you feel after drinking hot cocoa?

A: Marsh-mellow

Q: How do you know if there's a polar bear in your refrigerator?

A: The door won't close!

Q: How do alligators cook their Christmas dinner?

A: In a croc-pot

Q: What do you get when you cross a pine tree with a hyena?

A: An ever-grin tree

Q: What do you get if you put your head in the punch bowl?

A: Egg-noggin

Q: What's the best thing to drink on Christmas Eve?

A: Nativi-tea

Q: What do you get when you cross a squirrel and a Christmas pirate?

A: Treasure chestnuts roasting on an open fire

Q: What do you get when an astronaut goes skiing?

A: An ava-launch

Q: What did one skier say to the other skier?

A: "It's all downhill from here."

Q: What's Santa's favorite book?

A: *Merry Poppins*

Q: What kind of dinosaur hibernates for the winter?

A: A bronto-snore-us

Q: Why did the child need new glasses for Christmas?

A: He didn't have visions of sugarplums dancing in his head.

Q: What do reindeer have that no other animals have?

A: Baby reindeer

Q: Did you hear about the cat who chewed on the Christmas lights?

A: It was shocking!

Q: Did you hear about the Christmas star?

A: It's out of this world.

Q: Why couldn't the fish go Christmas shopping?

A: It didn't have anemone.

Q: How do you spell *frozen* with only three letters?

A: *I-C-E!*

Q: What kind of snowmobile does a farmer like to ride?

A: A Cow-asaki

Q: How does a grizzly get through the holidays?

A: He grins and bears it.

- -

Q: How did the wise men sneak across the desert?

A: They had camel-flage.

Q: What do you get when a polar bear sits on a pumpkin?

A: Squash

Q: How do you pay when you're Christmas shopping?

A: With jingle bills

Q: What kind of toy does a chicken want for Christmas?

A: A Jack-in-the-bok-bok-box!

Q: How does an opera singer make Christmas cookies?

A: With icing (I sing)

Brother: I broke my candy cane in two places.

Sister: Then don't go to those places anymore!

Julie: Did you have fun at the Christmas party?

Josie: No, it was a Feliz Navi-dud.

Q: How do you invite a fish to your Christmas party?

A: Drop it a line.

Q: What did Santa say when he parked his sleigh?

A: "There's snow place like home."

Q: Why did the snowman need dandruff shampoo?

A: Because he had snowflakes.

Knock, knock.

Who's there?

Window.

Window who?

Window you want to open your Christmas presents?

Q: Why did the girl give the boy an orange for Christmas?

A: Because he was her main squeeze.

Q: What do you get when you hang a turkey from the fireplace?

A: A stocking stuffer

Q: Why did the girl get celery for Christmas?

A: It was a stalk-ing stuffer.

Knock, knock.

Who's there?

Don.

Don who?

Don you want to come out and play in the snow?

- -

Knock, knock.

Who's there?

Sarah.

Sarah who?

Sarah reason you're not having any Christmas cookies?

Knock, knock.

Who's there?

Funnel.

Funnel who?

The funnel start once everyone shows up to the party!

Brother: Is this present from Mom?

Sister: Ap-parent-ly it is!

Q: What's a cow's favorite Christmas song?

A: "Jingle Bulls"

- -

Q: What is an elf's favorite dessert?

A: Shortbread cookies

Knock, knock.

> Who's there?

Braydon.

> Braydon who?

Are you Braydon your hair for the Christmas party?

Q: How does Santa get into his chalet?

A: With a s-key (ski)

Q: What do you put in a hyena's Christmas stocking?

A: A Snickers bar

Q: Why was the snowman so mean?

A: Because he was coldhearted.

Q: What do you get when you mix Rudolph and the queen?

A: A reign-deer

Knock, knock.

Who's there?

Police.

Police who?

Police come over for Christmas dinner!

Knock, knock.

Who's there?

Ice cream.

Ice cream who?

Ice cream when I see the abominable snowman!

Q: **What do you get when you combine a snowball, a fish, and a Christmas tree branch?**

A: A frozen fish stick

Knock, knock.

Who's there?

Megan.

Megan who?

It's Megan me crazy having to wait to open my presents!

Knock, knock.

Who's there?

Glove.

Glove who?

I glove the holidays.

Q: Why does Santa like his sleigh?

A: Because it's satis-flying.

Q: Why do reindeer eat so many candy canes?

A: For nourish-mint

Q: Why did the snowman get a headache?

A: He had brain freeze.

- -

Q: Why did Santa's reindeer go to jail?

A: For Comet-ting a crime

Q: What kind of dogs saw the Christmas star?

A: German shepherds

Q: Why couldn't the conductor drive the Polar Express?

A: He didn't have enough training.

Q: How do pirates save money on their Christmas shopping?

A: They look for sails.

Q: Why did Santa go back for more dessert?

A: Because he wanted to retreat.

Q: How does a sailor get to church on Christmas Eve?

A: On his wor-ship

Tongue Twisters

Round red wreath.

Striped stuffed stockings.

Green glitter glue.

Santa sings silly sleigh songs.

Q: Why did the dog always get depressed at Christmas?

A: Because the holidays were ruff.

Cassie: Did the cow like the present you got him?

Kendra: No, he thought it was udderly ridiculous.

Knock, knock.

Who's there?

Ville.

Ville who?

No, the opposite: it's Whoville.

Knock, knock.

Who's there?

Hammond.

Hammond who?

Hammond eggs taste great on

Christmas morning.

Q: Why was the farmer on Santa's naughty list?

A: Because his pig squealed on him!

Q: What do you call a twig that doesn't like Christmas?

A: A stick-in-the-mud

Q: How did the turkey get home for Christmas?

A: In a gravy boat

Q: Why do baseball players love Christmas dinner?

A: They like to be behind the plate.

- -

Q: What is a squirrel's favorite part of the Christmas season?

A: Going to see *The Nutcracker*

Billy: I got my pig some soap for Christmas.

Ben: That's hogwash!

Knock, knock.

Who's there?

Lion.

Lion who?

I'd be lion if I told you I didn't love the holidays.

Q: How do you make a strawberry shake?

A: Introduce it to the abominable snowman.

Knock, knock.

Who's there?

Weed.

Weed who?

Weed better leave for the Christmas party or we'll be late!

Knock, knock.

Who's there?

Kenya.

Kenya who?

Kenya tell me your favorite Christmas tradition?

Q: Why did the moon get sick after eating Christmas dinner?

A: Because it was so full.

Q: **Which baseball player makes the best Christmas cakes?**

A: The batter

Q: **How do the Christmas angels greet each other?**

A: They say, "Halo."

Q: **What happened when the rabbit ate too many Christmas cookies?**

A: It was hopped up on sugar.

Q: **Why don't crabs spend much money for Christmas?**

A: Because they're penny-pinchers.

Q: Why don't hyenas get sick in the winter?

A: Because laughter is the best medicine.

Sally: What if Jimmy can't play the trumpet in the Christmas concert?

Suzie: We'll find a substi-toot.

Q: Why did the boy hang triangles on his Christmas tree?

A: So he could have a geome-tree.

Q: What do reindeer like to eat with their spaghetti?

A: Meat-bells

Luke: Does Santa like to study chemistry?

Stew: Only periodically.

Knock, knock.

Who's there?

Dozen.

Dozen who?

Dozen anyone want to sing a Christmas carol?

Knock, knock.

Who's there?

Reindeer.

Reindeer who?

It's going to reindeer, so you'd better bring an umbrella.

Q: **Why do hummingbirds hum Christmas carols?**

A: Because they can't remember the words.

Q: **How do ducks celebrate New Year's Eve?**

A: With fire-quackers

Q: **What is something that's easy to catch in the winter, but hard to throw?**

A: A cold

Q: **Why did the raisin stay home from the Christmas party?**

A: Because it couldn't find a date.

Knock, knock.

Who's there?

Orange.

Orange who?

Orange you glad Christmas is almost here?

Q: What kind of fruit decorates a Christmas tree?

A: A pineapple

Q: Why did the orange stop Christmas shopping?

A: Because it ran out of juice.

Q: What do you get when your dog plays too long in the snow?

A: A pup-sicle

- -

Knock, knock.

Who's there?

Candice.

Candice who?

Candice holiday season get any better?

Knock, knock.

Who's there?

Juan.

Juan who?

Juan a kiss under the mistletoe?

Knock, knock.

Who's there?

Minnow.

Minnow who?

Let minnow if you can't make it to the Christmas party.

- -

Q: What happened when the cucumber ran out of wrapping paper?

A: It left him in a pickle.

Susie: Is your Christmas gift here yet?

Sally: Yes, it's present.

Caleb: Do you like the red frosting on my Christmas cookies?

Callie: Yes, it's to dye for.

Q: What does Santa use for a map?

A: A snow globe

- -

Q: Why do kids get bad grades during the holidays?

A: Because it's D-cember.

Q: What did Santa say when the elf told a funny joke?

A: "You sleigh me!"

Q: What do you give a rabbit for Christmas?

A: A hare-brush

Q: What do you give a flea for Christmas?

A: An Itch A Sketch

Q: Why did the boy get a bucket for Christmas?

A: Because he looked a little pail.

Stanley: Did your dad like the statue you gave him for Christmas?

Henry: No, it was a bust.

Eva: Did you know Santa's suit is exactly the right size?

Ava: Well, that's fitting.

Q: Why do snowmen wear sunglasses?

A: To keep the sun out of their ice.

- -

Anna: Should we get Dad a drill for Christmas?

Ella: No, that's boring.

Q: Why is Christmas so exciting?

A: Because it's an advent-ure.

Q: Why won't Santa wear an itchy scarf?

A: Because it's a pain in the neck.

Q: How did Santa feel about the house with the security system?

A: He was alarmed!

Q: Where did Noah like to go in the winter?

A: All the way to the ark-tic

- -

Q: How does Santa know what to give a zebra for Christmas?

A: The answer is black and white.

Josie: You forgot the lamb for the nativity scene!

Jamie: Well, I feel sheepish.

Q: Why can't Martians get along at Christmas?

A: Because they're alienated from one another.

Q: When is it hard to hear a Christmas movie?

A: When it's ani-muted

Q: How did Santa feel when he got soot on his suit?

A: He felt ash-amed.

Lucy: Are you allowed to make up a Christmas story?

Lena: Yes, I'm authorized.

Q: What does a ghost think about Christmas carols?

A: It thinks they're boo-tiful.

Q: How does a wolf like its Christmas cookies?

A: Bite-sized.

Tory: Why did Santa put tuna in my stocking?

Terry: He thought it would be bene-fish-ial.

Q: Why do elves like to go camping?

A: Because they're so compe-tent.

Q: Why don't we go camping in the winter?

A: Because it's too in-tents.

Q: How do you know when a snowman doesn't like you?

A: He'll give you the cold shoulder.

Jane: My mom won't let me embroider my Christmas stocking!

Jill: Well, that's crewel!

Q: Why did Mrs. Claus give Rudolph a hug?

A: Because he was so deer.

Q: Why was the beaver so sad at Christmas?

A: Because his present was dam-aged.

Q: Why did the elf have to clean up after the reindeer?

A: Because it was his doody.

Q: Why do cows like to sing Christmas carols?

A: Because they're so moo-sical.

Q: Why do elves always wear perfume?

A: They think it's e-scent-ial.

- -

Q: What did Luke Skywalker say at Christmas dinner?

A: "May the fork be with you."

Q: Why did Santa fly his sleigh through the Grand Canyon?

A: He thought it was gorge-ous.

Q: When does sledding make you laugh?

A: When it's hill-arious

Q: How do cows pay for their Christmas shopping?

A: With their moo-lah

- -

**Q: When can't you put any jelly in
your stocking?**

A: When it's already jam-packed.

**Q: Why shouldn't the reindeer make fun of
Rudolph's nose?**

A: Because it's impo-light.

Darla: When should we sing Christmas carols?

Debby: Hymn-ediately!

Q: Why is Santa so jolly?

A: Because he's a good fellow.

- -

Q: Which size cup of hot cocoa tastes the best?

A: A medi-yum

Mrs. Claus: I ironed your Santa suit for Christmas Eve.

Santa: I'm impressed!

Q: Why was the chef late for Christmas dinner?

A: He ran out of thyme.

Q: What do you call a great snowplow driver?

A: Wreckless

Q: What happens if you see a polar bear at the shopping center?

A: You might get mall-ed.

- -

Q: **How do you see an ice-cream cone from far away?**

A: Use a tele-scoop.

Q: **What does a hen have for dessert at Christmas?**

A: Layer cake

Q: **How did the wise men know to follow the star?**

A: They had frankin-sense.

Q: **How do you make your Christmas cards unique?**

A: You put your own stamp on them.

Q: Why were the reindeer mad at Santa?

A: He drove them up the wall.

Q: Why did two skunks give each other the same present?

A: Because great minds stink alike.

Q: Does Santa worry about delivering all the presents?

A: No, he's got it in the bag.

Q: How did the Three Little Pigs stay merry at Christmas?

A: They kept their chinny-chin-chins up.

- -

Q: When does Santa deliver presents to the sheep?

A: Last but not fleeced

Kelly: Will Santa bring my dog a present?

Karly: Make no bones about it.

Q: What did Santa say to the naughty squirrel?

A: "If you can't say something nice, don't say nuttin' at all."

Q: How did the canary afford all her Christmas gifts?

A: She used her nest egg.

Curtis: Are you excited to put up the Christmas tree?

Carter: Yes, I'm on pines and needles!

Gary: Is this star too fancy for our Christmas tree?

Mary: Yes, I think it's over-the-top.

Q: Why doesn't Blitzen ever get in trouble?

A: He's always passing the buck.

Q: Why is everyone happy at the North Pole?

A: Because they're on top of the world.

Q: Why does Santa keep a hammer in his sleigh on Christmas Eve?

A: So he can beat the clock.

- -

Q: When will Santa come down the chimney?

A: In the Nick of time

Q: When should you open your Christmas gifts?

A: There's no time like the present.

Q: Why won't you ever see the

gingerbread man cry?

A: Because he's one tough cookie.

Bobby: Santa makes you mad?

Billy: Yes, every time he's here I see red.

- -

Q: Why did the mittens get married?

A: It was glove at first sight.

Q: When do you bring lipstick under the mistletoe?

A: If you want to kiss and makeup.

Q: Why did the elf bring his garbage on a date to the movies?

A: He wanted to take out the trash.

Q: Where do you keep your Santa suit?

A: In the Santa Claus-et

- -

Q: When does a weatherman need an umbrella?

A: When his Christmas cookies have sprinkles

Q: Why did Santa hire an elephant for

his workshop?

A: Because it would work for peanuts.

Q: How does a chicken get to the

Christmas party?

A: In a heli-coop-ter

Q: Why did the pig look great at the

Christmas party?

A: Because it was so sty-lish.

- -

Q: How is a wool cardigan like a guy at the gym?

A: They're both heavy sweaters.

Q: Are the reindeer excited about the Christmas party?

A: Yes, they'll be there with bells on.

Grandma: Did Jimmy like the soccer ball I gave him for Christmas?

Grandpa: He got a kick out of it.

- -

Q: What do sharks eat for Christmas dessert?

A: Octo-pie

**Ralphie: Why did you give me lettuce
    for Christmas?**

Alfie: You said you wanted to get ahead.

**Q: How did Dorothy know what to give the
    Scarecrow for Christmas?**

A: It was a no-brainer.

**Q: Why did the boy keep asking for a train
    for Christmas?**

A: He had a one-track mind.

Q: What did the alien think about his Christmas present?

A: He thought it was out of this world.

Q: What do polar bears want for breakfast on Christmas morning?

A: Grrrr-nola

Q: What do you get when you cross a reindeer and a ghost?

A: A cari-boo

Knock, knock.

Who's there?

Alpine.

Alpine who?

Alpine trees look great with Christmas lights.

- -

Q: What did the pirate say when he was freezing in the snow?

A: "Shiver me timbers!"

Q: What game do you give a mouse for Christmas?

A: Par-cheesy

Q: Why can't ponies sing Christmas carols?

A: Because they're a little horse.

Toby: I ruined the treats for Christmas.

Tommy: Oh, fudge!

Q: When is a puppy like a cold winter's day?

A: When it's nippy

Q: Why did the Easter Bunny go trick-or-treating at Christmas?

A: He was in a holi-daze.

Q: Why would you give away a fireplace for free?

A: You must have a big hearth.

Q: What happens if you give a snowman a carrot?

A: He'll get nosy.

Q: Why won't penguins use cell phones?

A: Because they're cold-fashioned.

Q: What do you call Santa when his suit is wrinkled?

A: Kris Krinkle

Sara: Why won't your parents eat almonds at Christmastime?

Dora: They're nuts.

Q: What will happen if you run out of peppermints?

A: People will raise cane!

Q: Why was Santa sad?

A: He didn't think his parents believed in him.

Q: Why couldn't Rudolph buy any more soap?

A: He was all washed-up.

- -

Q: What did the snowplow driver say at the end of the season?

A: "It was nice snowing you."

Q: What's a turkey's favorite Christmas dessert?

A: Bluberry gobbler

Q: Why couldn't the elf pay for her Christmas shopping?

A: She was a little short.

- -

Q: What happened when the reindeer flew into a mountain?

A: They couldn't get over it.

Knock, knock.

Who's there?

Alpaca.

Alpaca who?

Alpaca bag and visit Grandma for Christmas.

Q: Why shouldn't you do homework while you're ice-skating?

A: Your grades might slip.

Jeremy: Why do you believe in Santa Claus?

Jillian: Because the Easter Bunny and the tooth fairy told me he's real.

- -

Q: What did the rabbit say to the frog?

A: "Hoppy Holidays!"

Wyatt: Did you hear we're just

having sandwiches for Christmas dinner?

William: That's a bunch of baloney!

Q: What does a frog say when it's unwrapping

its Christmas presents?

A: "Rip it, rip it, rip it."

Q: Why wouldn't the skeleton go snowboarding

down the mountain?

A: He didn't have the guts.

- -

Olivia: Did you know lots of reindeer live in Alaska?

Violet: That's what I herd.

Aunt Sue: Is Alex disappointed that he caught a cold at Christmas?

Uncle Sam: He'll get over it.

Bess: Do you like the trampoline Santa gave you for Christmas?

Tess: I'm jumping for joy!

Q: Why was the dog barking at the fireplace?

A: It made him hot under the collar.

Tracy: Was your mom surprised when she got a rug for Christmas?

Trudy: She was floored!

Q: Why did Santa give Humpty Dumpty a lot of presents?

A: Because he's a good egg.

Q: Why did the snowman take a carrot to the library?

A: So he could put his nose in a book.

Q: How is Santa's beard like a Christmas tree?

A: They both need trimming.

Q: **When does King Arthur do his Christmas shopping?**

A: At knight

Q: **How do dogs play Christmas carols?**

A: On a trombone

Q: **Why was the cookie so excited to see its family at Christmas?**

A: Because it was a wafer such a long time.

Q: **Why did the hotdog keep telling jokes at the Christmas talent show?**

A: Because it was on a roll.

Q: Why did the snowman go to the dentist?

A: He wanted his teeth whitened.

Q: What happens when a polar bear is all alone?

A: He's feels ice-olated.

**Peter: Do you think we should read a
Christmas story?**

Tyler: That's a novel idea!

**Q: What happened when the elf showed up to
work in flip-flops?**

A: Santa gave him the boot!

- -

Knock, knock.

Who's there?

Europe.

Europe who?

Europe late waiting for Santa Claus!

Q: What kind of bird is sad when Christmas is over?

A: A bluebird

Q: Why was the elf yelling?

A: Because he stubbed his mistletoe.

Knock, knock.

Who's there?

Cook.

Cook who?

Clearly the holidays are making you a little crazy!

Knock, knock.

Who's there?

Avery.

Avery who?

Avery nice person wished me Merry Christmas today.

Q: What game do elves like to play when they're not making toys?

A: Gift tag

- -

Knock, knock.

Who's there?

Abby.

Abby who?

Abby New Year!

Q: How do snowmen make friends at parties?

A: They know how to break the ice.

Q: How do you get a polar bear's attention?

A: With a cold snap

Knock, knock.

Who's there?

Figs.

Figs who?

Can you figs the star on the Christmas tree?

Q: Why do you sing lullabies to a snowbank?

A: So it can drift off to sleep.

Tony: I don't think we'll finish our Christmas story on time.

Tammy: We'll have to book it!

Knock, knock.

Who's there?

Jewel.

Jewel who?

Jewel feel sick if you eat too many candy canes.

- -

Knock, knock.

Who's there?

Left hand.

Left hand who?

I left hand forgot my scarf and mittens.

Knock, knock.

Who's there?

Wendy.

Wendy who?

Wendy snow falls, we can go sledding.

Knock, knock.

Who's there?

Sticker.

Sticker who?

Sticker presents under the tree before

Christmas Eve!

Knock, knock.

Who's there?

Rooster.

Rooster who?

Rooster turkey in the oven for

Christmas dinner.

Knock, knock.

Who's there?

Firewood.

Firewood who?

A firewood warm things up in here.